Other titles in this series:
Barnaby's Cuckoo Clock
Flipperty's Aeroplane
Larry's Caravan

ISBN 0-86163-231-1

Copyright © 1988 Award Publications Limited

First published 1988
Fourth impression 1992

Published by Award Publications Limited,
Spring House, Spring Place,
Kentish Town, London NW5 3BH

Printed in Singapore

TUFTY'S POT
OF PAINT

Written and illustrated
by
Rene Cloke

AWARD PUBLICATIONS

LONDON

"I think I will paint the front door," said
Tufty, the squirrel, "it is looking very shabby."

"Yes," agreed Hazel, "all the other squirrels'
houses in Hopping Wood are looking fresh and
bright with yellow, blue or green doors. What
colour will you paint ours?"

Tufty looked around. The blue and green doors
were pretty and the yellow ones looked as though
the sun was shining on them even on wet days, but
he wanted to be different.

"Let's have a red door," he said.

Bertha and Barnaby Bunny's shop was on the other side of the river which ran through Hopping Wood so, carrying his basket, Tufty went down to the boathouse where he kept his boat.

As he pushed off from the bank, Flipperty Frog called out to him –

"The blackberries are ripe on Willow Island, why don't you gather some?"

"I'll stop for some on the way back,"answered Tufty.

He rowed across the river and pulled up his boat on the other side.

There were quite a lot of people in the little shop in the roots of the oak tree.

The shop sold *almost* everything.

Dumpling, the black piglet, and Merry, the kitten, from Hopping Wood Farm had come to buy biscuits and chocolate. Two baby rabbits were being fitted with shoes and Dulcie Duck wanted a saucepan and two boxes of matches.

Tufty looked at the tins of paint.

There were such lovely colours to choose from that he spent quite a long time making up his mind. At last he decided on POPPY RED and bought a big paint brush as well.

Then he bought a pound of apples to cook with the blackberries he hoped to pick.

The little rabbits had chosen their shoes and Dulcie Duck had waddled off with her saucepan and matches.

"I'm going to paint the front door," Tufty told Dumpling and Merry, "but first I'm going to gather some blackberries on Willow Island as I cross the river."

"May we come with you?" asked Merry and Dumpling. "There's plenty of room for blackberries in our basket."

So the three little animals trotted through
the wood and down to the river where Tufty had left
his boat.

Dumpling was so fat that there was not much
room for the other two and he was so heavy that
Tufty found it hard work rowing to Willow
Island in the middle of the river.

At last they reached
the island and were soon
busily picking the lovely
ripe blackberries.

Dumpling said he was so hungry that he must
eat a few first – then he ate a few more.

Merry scrambled high and low amongst the
bushes and collected quite a lot of blackberries
in her basket. Tufty was able to run along the
high branches and pick the biggest and ripest fruit.

But when they had filled their baskets and were ready to go home, they had a big surprise.

The boat had drifted away!

"What shall we do?" mewed Merry.

"Shall we have to stay here for ever?" asked Dumpling, wondering how long he could enjoy eating nothing but blackberries, chocolate and biscuits.

Tufty could see his boat
drifting along by the bank –
it looked a long way off.

"Let's all shout for help,"
said Dumpling. So they mewed
and squeaked and grunted but
they could not make much
noise and nobody heard them.

"I wish we could swim,"
said Merry.

"I wish we had more food,"
said Dumpling.

"I wish we had a flag to
wave," said Tufty, "someone
might see it from the shore."

"We could wave my scarf,"
said Merry, "It's a big one
but it won't show very well,
it's pale blue."

Tufty tried waving the
scarf but no one came.

"We ought to have a red flag," said Dumpling, "someone would be sure to see that."

"That gives me an idea!" cried Tufty. He ran to the spot where they had landed and found the pot of red paint and the paint brush which he had taken from his basket when he had started to gather blackberries.

"Give me your scarf, Merry."
Tufty laid it on the ground, opened the tin
and, dipping his brush in the paint, spread the lovely
red colour all over the scarf.

"A red flag!"
cried Dumpling "Hurrah!"
"Now," said Tufty,
"I'll climb up this tree and
you must hand me the
flag."

Up he went and
Merry climbed up after
him.

Dumpling handed
her the flag and she
passed it to Tufty.

Tufty climbed to the
very top of the tree.

"There's Larry!" squeaked the little squirrel as he saw the puppy from Hopping Wood Farm wandering along the river bank.

Tufty waved the red-painted scarf above his head,

"I do hope he will see our flag!"

And Larry did.

He was very surprised but he soon saw what had happened. He waved a paw to his friends, then, diving into the river, he swam towards the island, pulling the boat after him.

Tufty, Merry and Dumpling were very pleased
to be rescued. They gave Larry some of the
biscuits.

"We thought we should have to stay here for
ever," said Dumpling, "and live on blackberries."

Larry looked at the painted scarf.

"That makes a very fine flag," he said as he munched his biscuits, "but it will be rather sticky for a scarf."

Tufty read the label on the tin.

"It's quick-drying paint," he said.

Then the squirrel, the piglet and the kitten got into the boat and Larry towed them to the bank near the farm.

"Goodbye, Tufty! goodbye!" cried the three farmyard friends as they scampered off to Hopping Wood Farm.

"Goodbye!" Tufty called as he started to row back across the river, "I must hurry home with my apples and blackberries. Hazel will wonder where I am."

Hazel *did* wonder.
"You have been a long
time buying a tin of paint!"
she said as Tufty came
running through the wood.

When Tufty painted the front door the next day
he had to leave a bare patch as there was not
quite enough paint.

"That's because you painted the scarf with
some of the paint," said Hazel.

"Never mind," said Tufty, " we'll pretend it's meant to look like that." and he wrote the name of their house on the bare space –

THE NUT HUT

Hazel Squirrel was
delighted with the blackberries.
She made six pounds
of blackberry and apple
jelly and a big pie.

Then she invited the other
animals to a party.

They all admired the beautiful red door of the squirrels' house and they enjoyed the blackberry and apple jelly and ate large pieces of the pie.

Merry, Dumpling and Tufty had a most exciting time telling all their friends about their adventure.

But they didn't want it to happen again so they planned to have swimming lessons in the duck pond.

Dumpling said the water looked too cold and wet.

The only person who was not pleased was Merry's mother. She said that the pale blue scarf was a new one and would never look the same again.